Danger!

Jessica, Elizabeth, and Eva sneaked into the Pearces' backyard. "Double, double, toil and trouble! Fire burn, and cauldron bubble!" they heard someone chant.

"Caroline's casting a spell!" Eva whispered. "We've got to get a closer look."

Jessica pulled on Elizabeth's arm. "I say we get out of here."

Just then Caroline poked her head out of the garage. "What are you doing here?" she asked. "You're spying on me, aren't you?"

Elizabeth gulped. "Are—are you a good witch?"

"No, I'm a wicked witch," Caroline said. "The most wicked witch in the whole school! And don't you forget it!"

Elizabeth took a few steps back. Caroline had just admitted that she was a witch!

Bantam Books in the SWEET VALLEY KIDS series

SWEET VALLEY KIDS

CAROLINE'S HALLOWEEN SPELL

Written by
Molly Mia Stewart

Created by
FRANCINE PASCAL

Illustrated by
Ying-Hwa Hu

A BANTAM BOOK®
NEW YORK·TORONTO·LONDON·SYDNEY·AUCKLAND

To Gabriel Allon Goldstein

RL 2, 005-008

CAROLINE'S HALLOWEEN SPELL
A Bantam Book / October 1992

*Sweet Valley High® and Sweet Valley Kids are
trademarks of Francine Pascal*

Conceived by Francine Pascal

*Produced by Daniel Weiss Associates, Inc.
33 West 17th Street
New York, NY 10011*

Cover art by Susan Tang

ISBN: 0-553-48006-5

Published simultaneously in the United States and Canada

Bantam Books are published by Bantam Books, a division of Bantam
Doubleday Dell Publishing Group, Inc. Its trademark, consisting of the
words "Bantam Books" and the portrayal of a rooster, is Registered in
U.S. Patent and Trademark Office and in other countries. Marca Regis-
trada. Bantam Books, 1540 Broadway, New York, New York 10036.

PRINTED IN THE UNITED STATES OF AMERICA

CWO   0 9 8 7 6 5 4 3

CHAPTER 1

Caroline's Threat

"Only four more days until Halloween," Jessica Wakefield said. It was Friday morning.

Jessica's twin sister, Elizabeth, smiled. "I love Halloween costumes," she said.

"Me, too," said Caroline Pearce. Caroline was sitting in the bus seat behind Elizabeth and Jessica. She lived down the street from the twins.

"I love jack-o-lanterns," Elizabeth said, smiling at Caroline. Most of Elizabeth's friends didn't like Caroline very much because she was a tattletale, but Elizabeth always tried to be nice to her.

"I love haunted houses," Jessica said.

"I love trick-or-treating," Elizabeth and Jessica said at exactly the same time. Then they both laughed.

Jessica and Elizabeth often said things at exactly the same time. That wasn't surprising because Elizabeth and Jessica weren't just twins—they were identical twins.

Both girls had blue-green eyes and long, blond hair with bangs. When they wore matching outfits, most of their second-grade classmates had trouble telling them apart.

But although Jessica and Elizabeth looked the same on the outside, they were very different on the inside. Elizabeth enjoyed school, and she loved to read and to write stories. She was proud to play on a team in the Sweet Valley Soccer League.

Jessica didn't like playing sports because she hated getting her clothes dirty. She preferred to stay inside with her dolls and stuffed animals. She didn't like school very much, and she liked talking to her friends more than reading books.

Even though Jessica and Elizabeth had different interests, they were best friends. Being twins was special to them. They sat next to each other in Mrs. Otis's class at school, and they shared a bedroom at home. They knew they would be best friends forever.

"What are you going to be for Halloween?" Elizabeth asked Caroline.

"You tell me what you're going to be first,"

Caroline said, pushing back her shoulder-length red hair.

"I don't know yet. I haven't thought of anything really good," Elizabeth answered.

"I'm going to be a cheerleader," Jessica announced. "With pompoms and everything."

"So what are you going to be, Caroline?" Elizabeth asked again.

Caroline shook her head. "It's none of your business," she said. She leaned back and crossed her arms. "You'll find out on Halloween."

Winston Egbert leaned across the aisle. "I bet Caroline *forgot* what she's going to be," he teased. "Her brain must be rusting." He pointed to Caroline's red hair. "See? Her whole head is rusty!"

Jessica giggled.

Todd Wilkins was sharing a seat with Winston. "I'd rather be dead than red in the head," Todd sang loudly.

"Hey, Caroline," Charlie Cashman yelled from the back of the bus. "I think you ate too many carrots."

Caroline frowned. She hated to be teased. "Cut it out, you guys."

"Yeah, quit it," Elizabeth said. "It's not nice."

Jessica didn't understand why her sister was sticking up for Caroline. She thought the boys were funny. "Caroline, do something quick," she said. "Your hair is on fire!"

Caroline's face turned redder than her hair. She looked furious. "If you don't stop, you'll be sorry," she yelled at Jessica and the boys.

"Oh no," Charlie said jokingly. "I'm scared."

Winston, Todd, and Jessica laughed.

Caroline crossed her arms. "You will be sorry," she said. "Just you wait."

CHAPTER 2

Real Witches

That morning in homeroom, all anyone could talk about was Halloween. "I'm going to be a clown," Eva Simpson told the twins. "My mom made me a great costume. It has big polka dots all over it, and a ruffled collar. I'm going to wear a big red fake nose and a bright green wig, and paint my face with sparkles."

"That sounds great," Elizabeth said. "You'll be ready to join the circus."

"I'm going to be a dog," Amy Sutton said. "I've been practicing my bark. Ruff! Ruff!"

Just then Charlie galloped over on an

imaginary horse. He was going to be a cowboy for Halloween. "Git along, little doggie!" he yelled. He galloped to the other side of the classroom, where Kisho Murasaki and Winston were having a pretend sword fight. Both of them were going to be pirates.

Their teacher, Mrs. Otis, walked into the room and clapped her hands. "OK, everybody. Let's try to calm down."

For a few seconds, the class was quiet. Then Elizabeth heard Lila Fowler whisper something to Jessica. Soon, everyone was talking again.

"I'm glad you're all thinking about your Halloween costumes," Mrs. Otis said over the noise. "Don't forget to wear them to school on Tuesday for the Best Class Costume contest."

"I hope I win," Elizabeth whispered to Amy.

"Ruff! Me, too," Amy replied.

"Since we're talking about Halloween, I want to tell you all about your special Halloween assignment," Mrs. Otis said. "We're going to the library in a few minutes. When we get there, I want each of you to check out a book about Halloween. On Tuesday you'll give your book reports in front of the class."

Elizabeth smiled. A Halloween book report sounded like fun. She couldn't wait to start working on hers. Elizabeth already knew what she wanted to write about— witches.

"Maybe you can get an idea for a Halloween costume in the library," Jessica whispered to her sister as everyone got in line to go down the hall to the library.

"Good idea," Elizabeth whispered back.

When they got to the library, Jessica and

Elizabeth headed for the special display case. This month all the student artwork and poems in the case were about Halloween. Next to the display were several long shelves full of books having to do with the holiday. Elizabeth started reading the titles. She soon found a book called *All About Witches*.

"Look," Jessica said, pulling a book off the shelf as well. She read the title out loud. "*How Halloween Started*. I never thought about that before. Do you know, Liz?"

Elizabeth shook her head. "No. It'll make a great report."

"If you found a book, Jess, come help me," Lila called to Jessica. "I can't decide what to read about."

As Jessica went to help Lila, Elizabeth sat down on the library couch and started reading her book. She read that people used to

think that women and girls with red hair were witches. Elizabeth thought that was silly. Everyone knew that there was no such thing as a real witch.

But reading about red hair reminded Elizabeth of Caroline. Elizabeth wanted to tell Caroline that she was sorry Jessica had teased her. Elizabeth looked around the library. She saw Caroline sitting at a table by herself, turning the pages of a thick, dusty old book. Elizabeth got up and walked over to her.

"Hi, Caroline. What are you looking at?" Elizabeth asked.

"Nothing," Caroline said. She closed the book and hid it under the table so that Elizabeth couldn't see the title.

Elizabeth was surprised. *Caroline sure is acting strange*, she thought. *I wonder if she has a secret?*

CHAPTER 3

The Spooky Skeleton

"Let's play on the jungle gym," Jessica said at recess.

"OK, I'll race you there," Elizabeth said. She ran off, with Jessica close behind her.

Seconds later, Jessica took the lead and tagged one of the jungle gym's metal bars. "I win!" she yelled.

"Hey, Jessica," Kisho called from his seat on a high bar. "Maybe you should be a track star for Halloween."

Amy was hanging upside down from a lower bar. "And Elizabeth could be a tortoise," she said.

"You'd better watch out," Elizabeth said with a smile, as she swung her feet up on the bar next to Amy. "I'm thinking about being a witch. I might cast a spell on you!"

"You don't know anything about witches," Caroline shouted. She was sitting on the tire swing next to the jungle gym.

"Elizabeth knows more than you any day," Jessica answered loudly. She turned to her sister and shook her head. "Caroline is such a baby."

"Forget her," Kisho said. "My dad brought home a pumpkin yesterday. We're going to make a jack-o-lantern tonight."

"Halloween decorations are the greatest," Jessica said. She climbed to the top of the jungle gym and sat down next to Kisho. "There's a woman who lives down the street

15

from us who hangs up a huge scary skeleton every year. Her name is Mrs. Frankel."

Elizabeth pulled herself upright and started to climb up to where Kisho and Jessica were sitting. "Mrs. Frankel's skeleton *is* awfully spooky," she agreed. "It even glows in the dark."

Jessica shivered. "Maybe Mrs. Frankel does, too."

"Is Mrs. Frankel spooky?" Amy asked.

"She lives all alone in an old house," Elizabeth said. "She looks as if she's at least one hundred years old."

Jessica nodded. "And our brother, Steven, says she gobbles up little kids for breakfast."

"Every Halloween when we're trick-or-treating we dare each other to ring her bell," Elizabeth said.

"Nobody ever wants to," Jessica added.

"But it's worth it when we do," Elizabeth said. "Mrs. Frankel gives out the best candy in the whole neighborhood. Last year we got lots of chocolate bars, big bags of caramel popcorn, and some bubble gum."

"Mrs. Frankel isn't going to hang up a skeleton this year," Caroline announced. She had gotten off the tire swing and was standing at the bottom of the jungle gym. "She's going to hang up a ghost."

Jessica frowned. "How would you know what Mrs. Frankel is going to do?" she asked.

"I know lots of things," Caroline said, sounding mysterious. "You'll see."

"Caroline's just saying that to make you mad," Elizabeth whispered to Jessica. "She's trying to get back at you for teasing her."

18

Jessica frowned again. "You're probably right," she said to Elizabeth. "Let's just ignore her. There's no way Mrs. Frankel is going to hang up a boring old ghost!"

CHAPTER 4

The Ghost

That day after school, Elizabeth was still trying to decide what to be for Halloween.

"How about a dinosaur?" Jessica suggested as the twins walked home from the bus stop.

"Ken Matthews is going to be a dinosaur," Elizabeth said.

"An astronaut?" Jessica asked.

"No," Elizabeth said. "Todd was one last year. I want something different."

"A ballerina?" Jessica tried again.

Elizabeth shook her head.

"How about—"

"A ghost!" Elizabeth said suddenly. She stopped walking and stood frozen on the sidewalk.

"A ghost?" Jessica asked. "Ghosts are boring. I thought you said you wanted something different."

Elizabeth grabbed Jessica's arm and pointed at Mrs. Frankel's house. "Look!" she said.

Jessica gasped. A ghost was hanging on Mrs. Frankel's door. "Caroline was right," Jessica exclaimed.

Elizabeth nodded. She was positive that nothing had been hanging on Mrs. Frankel's door that morning. But somehow Caroline had known Mrs. Frankel would hang up a ghost instead of a skeleton.

Elizabeth thought about the library book she had checked out. It said people used to believe that women and girls with red hair were witches. What if it were true? Maybe Caroline was a witch! Elizabeth felt a shiver run up her back.

"Stupid ghost," Jessica said. "It's not scary at all."

Elizabeth knew Jessica was disappointed that Mrs. Frankel hadn't put up the glow-in-the-dark skeleton. But Elizabeth had more important things to worry about.

"My library book says witches can see into the future," Elizabeth said. "Jess, do you think Caroline is a—a witch?"

"No. That's silly. There're no such things as witches," Jessica said. "Mrs. Frankel probably told Caroline about the ghost."

Elizabeth's eyes widened. Mrs. Frankel never opened the dark shutters on her windows. The gate on her fence squeaked when the wind blew. Most kids wouldn't dream of talking to Mrs. Frankel, even on a dare.

"You mean you think Caroline *talked* to Mrs. Frankel?" Elizabeth said.

Jessica looked at her sister and swallowed. "Yes," she said softly. "How else would Caroline have known?"

Elizabeth stared at the ghost on Mrs. Frankel's door. She remembered how mysterious Caroline had acted at the library. Maybe Caroline was hiding a secret—a *big* secret. Maybe her secret was that she was a *real* witch.

"I'm going home, Liz," Jessica said. "This is scary." She started to march toward their house.

Suddenly, Elizabeth felt like running all the way home and locking the door after her.

"Wait up," she called after Jessica. "I'm coming, too!"

CHAPTER 5

A Broom, a Potion, and a Lizard

"Hurry up, Elizabeth," Jessica said on Saturday morning as she stuffed a forkful of scrambled eggs into her mouth. "It's time to go spying."

Jessica couldn't wait to put her latest plan into action. After the twins had seen Mrs. Frankel's ghost the day before, they had spent a long time talking about Caroline. They had gone out to the fort Elizabeth had built in the backyard so that the rest of the family wouldn't hear them. Elizabeth didn't want anyone else to know she thought Caroline was a witch until she had proof.

Jessica still wasn't convinced that Elizabeth's suspicions were right. But she had suggested that they spy on Caroline to see if they could find more evidence.

"OK, I guess I'm ready," Elizabeth said. She put her breakfast dishes in the sink and followed Jessica out the back door.

The twins ran down the street to Caroline's house. Then they sneaked into her backyard and hid behind an oak tree. A few minutes later, Caroline came out of the garage. She was carrying a broom.

Elizabeth gasped and looked at Jessica. "Witches use brooms to fly," she whispered.

"Does it say that in your book?" Jessica asked.

"No, but everyone knows that," Elizabeth replied.

Jessica looked doubtful. "I don't think that proves she's a witch, though."

Caroline crossed the yard and disappeared into the house. Jessica and Elizabeth looked around to make sure no one was in sight. Then they carefully sneaked up to the house and peered into the Pearces' kitchen window.

Inside they saw Caroline stirring a huge steaming pot.

"A magic potion," Elizabeth whispered, wide-eyed. "Witches make them all the time."

"Is *that* in your book?" Jessica asked.

"Yes," Elizabeth said, forgetting to whisper.

"Shh," Jessica whispered. "Caroline will hear us."

Elizabeth lowered her voice. "Witches make magic potions in big, black pots just like the one Caroline's using."

"She could be making anything in that pot," Jessica pointed out. But the way Elizabeth kept talking about witches was giving her the creeps. Jessica suddenly felt like getting far away from Caroline—just in case.

Inside the house, Caroline picked up the broom and walked out of the kitchen.

"What should we do now?" Elizabeth asked.

"Go home," Jessica said firmly. "Mom and Dad are taking us to the mall to shop for our Halloween costumes."

"Right," Elizabeth agreed. She grabbed her sister's hand and the two of them ran out of the Pearces' yard as fast as they could.

*   *   *

"We're ready to go, Mom," Jessica said once they walked into their own house.

"Sort of," Elizabeth added. She still hadn't decided what to be for Halloween.

"Don't worry, Elizabeth," Mrs. Wakefield said. "You'll see so many costumes you like that I bet it'll be hard to choose just one."

Once the Wakefields got to the mall, they went straight to a tiny costume store called Abracadabra. There were lots of people there shopping for Halloween costumes.

Mrs. Wakefield helped Jessica find a pair of pompoms for her cheerleading costume. The twins' older brother, Steven, started searching for a perfect pair of fangs. Steven was going to dress as a vampire for Halloween.

"Come on, Dad," Elizabeth said. "I need some help." Elizabeth had already looked at

29

several costume racks but nothing had caught her eye. She led her father to a counter that sold monster masks, jeweled crowns, magic wands, and long plastic fingernails.

"Do you see anything you like?" Mr. Wakefield asked. Elizabeth shook her head.

"Look over here," Jessica called from the other side of the store. Elizabeth and Mr. Wakefield hurried over. Jessica was standing in front of a counter that sold top hats, alien ears, plastic pig noses, and elephant trunks.

Elizabeth tried on a pair of alien ears but she didn't like the way they looked. Besides, she knew that Andy Franklin dressed up as an alien every year.

"I don't think I'll ever find a costume," Elizabeth said sadly.

Then Jessica picked up an oversized magnifying glass. "Hey, I have an idea!" She started whispering into Elizabeth's ear.

"Perfect!" Elizabeth said after Jessica explained her idea. Elizabeth suddenly looked much happier.

A few minutes later, the Wakefields left Abracadabra. Elizabeth had a big shopping bag in her hand and a big smile on her face.

"I think we earned an ice cream cone," Mrs. Wakefield said.

"All right!" the twins shouted at exactly the same time.

"I'm getting a double scoop of chocolate marshmallow chip," Steven announced as they walked by the pet store.

"I want . . ." Jessica didn't finish her sentence because Caroline and Mr. Pearce were just coming out of the shop. Caroline was carrying a big box that said "Pete's Pets" on the side. When she saw Jessica and Elizabeth, Caroline tried to hide the box behind her back.

"Hello, Mr. Pearce," Mrs. Wakefield said. "Hello, Caroline."

Mr. Wakefield smiled at Caroline. "Did you buy something for Halloween, Caroline?"

"None of your business," Caroline said quickly.

"Caroline!" Mr. Pearce said sternly. "That was very rude. Show the Wakefields what we bought."

Looking unhappy, Caroline slowly opened her box. When the Wakefields peered inside they saw that it contained a lizard.

"Excellent!" Steven said. He put his hand in the box and petted the reptile.

"Witches use lizards in their magic potions," Elizabeth whispered to Jessica.

"Really?" Jessica took a step back from the box. "Does it say so in your book?"

Elizabeth nodded.

Jessica bit her lip. She hated to admit it, but she was beginning to think that Elizabeth was right. All the evidence so far was showing that Caroline really was a witch.

CHAPTER 6

A Witch's Cat

The next day, the twins decided to go bike riding. As they were riding down their street, Jessica put her feet down so that her bike skidded to a stop right in front of Mrs. Frankel's house.

"What are you doing?" Elizabeth asked, stopping her bike behind Jessica's.

Jessica smiled and pointed to Mrs. Frankel's garden. "I dare you to knock on Mrs. Frankel's door and then run away."

Elizabeth looked at Mrs. Frankel's yard. The dry grass was taller than she was. Three overgrown willow trees hid most of the windows. The house's white paint was old and peeling off in big chunks. The cobble-stoned pathway leading up to Mrs. Frankel's door was being pushed up by the weeds growing under it.

Mrs. Frankel didn't have a doorbell. Instead, she had an old-fashioned knocker in the shape of a lion's head. Elizabeth could remember the sound Mrs. Frankel's door made when it opened on Halloween night: *CRRREEEAKKKK!* The thought gave Elizabeth goosebumps.

"I double dare you, Lizzie," Jessica said.

"Darers go first," Elizabeth said.

Jessica shook her head. "I'm not crazy. Even Steven won't go—"

"Shhh!" Elizabeth said suddenly. "I think I heard something."

Elizabeth and Jessica held their breath. The seconds ticked by.

"What did you hear?" Jessica asked finally.

"A sound," Elizabeth said. "There it is again!" She saw Jessica's eyes get big. This time Jessica had heard it, too.

"Come here," called a voice from Mrs. Frankel's garden. "You don't have to be afraid. Come here. Come here. Come here."

"I think—" Elizabeth's throat was dry. "I think Mrs. Frankel is coming to get us."

"Let's go—now," Jessica whispered.

Quickly and quietly the twins put their feet back onto their bicycle pedals and got ready to push off. But it was too late—the branches in Mrs. Frankel's garden had already started to shake. Whoever or whatever was in there was coming to get them.

Elizabeth wanted to pedal away but she was too scared to move. She squeezed her eyes shut and waited.

"Hi, Elizabeth. Hi, Jessica," said a familiar voice.

Elizabeth opened her eyes and saw Caroline crawling out of Mrs. Frankel's bushes. With one hand, she was brushing dirt off her knees, and with the other she was holding her cat.

"What were you doing in there?" Jessica asked.

"I was just—" Caroline started. She looked over her shoulder, back at Mrs. Frankel's yard. She looked nervous. "Just—"

Caroline's cat Misty was meowing. She didn't sound happy.

"Caroline!" Mr. Pearce called from down the street. "Lunchtime!"

"I've got to go," Caroline said, sounding relieved. She hurried down the street.

"Witches have cats," Elizabeth whispered, as the twins watched Caroline run off.

"Misty isn't black," Jessica pointed out.

"But what was Caroline *doing* in there?" Elizabeth asked.

Jessica shivered. "Good question."

Elizabeth thought for a moment. "I bet she was taking a lesson from Mrs. Frankel—a lesson on how to be a witch!"

CHAPTER 7

The Blackout

O n Monday morning, Elizabeth and Jessica were looking out of the classroom window. Heavy clouds hung in the sky. It was as dark as night outside.

"I don't believe it," Elizabeth said.

"It's a disaster," Jessica agreed.

Amy joined the twins at the window. "It's going to pour any second," she said. "Maybe there'll even be thunder and lightning."

"I hope not," Elizabeth said.

Lois Waller peeked over Amy's head. "Don't worry. It *couldn't* rain on Halloween."

"I know," Elizabeth said. "But what if it does?"

"Halloween would be ruined," Ellen Riteman said, walking over.

"We wouldn't be able to go trick-or-treating," Jessica said.

"We'd have to stay home in our costumes," Elizabeth added.

Mrs. Otis came over and looked out the window, too. "What perfect pre-Halloween weather," she said, smiling.

Elizabeth, Jessica, Amy, Ellen, and Lois turned around and stared at their teacher.

"What do you mean?" Amy asked.

"Well, Halloween is supposed to be spooky," Mrs. Otis said. "This type of weather creates the right mood. I'm sure witches and goblins feel right at home."

Jessica smiled. "Vampires would *love* this weather," she said.

"Yes," Amy agreed. "So would ghosts."

"And dragons and werewolves," Ellen added.

"And warlocks," Elizabeth said. "Warlocks are boy witches. I read about them in my library book."

Mrs. Otis laughed. "Why don't you all sit down. It's time for art."

Ken Matthews went to the supply closet and handed out black pipe cleaners and construction paper to everyone in the class. Then Mrs. Otis showed them how to make Halloween spiders. Twice while she was speaking, a big bolt of lightning and a rumble of thunder interrupted her.

Jessica looked out the window and bit her lip. Witches, goblins, and vampires might like thunder and lightning, but she was a little bit afraid of it.

"Look," Todd exclaimed. "It's raining."

Everyone ran to the windows.

There was an enormous clap of thunder. Suddenly all of the lights went out.

Ellen and Lila screamed.

"Everyone, sit down on the floor right where you are," Mrs. Otis said.

Jessica took Elizabeth's hand and squeezed it. Together, they slid down onto the floor.

"I'm afraid," Lois said. She sounded as if she was about to cry.

Then, the twins heard laughter. It was a shrill laugh that made their skin crawl.

"Why is Caroline laughing?" Jessica whispered to her sister. "It's scary without the lights."

"You guys are babies," Caroline said loudly. "Only little kids are afraid of the dark. I bet you all sleep with night lights on."

"Caroline, that's enough," Mrs. Otis said sternly.

"You're really not scared?" Julie Porter asked Caroline in a quivery voice.

"No, I'm just bored," Caroline answered. "I wish the lights would come on so that I could finish my spider."

Just then, the lights did come on.

"Well, that didn't last long," Mrs. Otis said. "Let's finish our Halloween projects."

"I believe you now," Jessica whispered to Elizabeth as they took their seats. "I think Caroline definitely is a witch. She just made the lights come back on!"

Elizabeth nodded. "That's what I think, too."

"What are you talking about?" Amy asked.

"Caroline," Jessica said in a hushed voice. "She's a witch. A *real* witch."

Amy looked surprised, so Elizabeth told her about the broom, the steaming potion, the lizard, and seeing Caroline crawl out of Mrs. Frankel's garden. By the time Elizabeth finished, Lila, Ellen, and Eva had gathered around to listen, too.

"My library book says witches have cat eyes," Elizabeth finished up. "That means they can see in the dark. I bet that's why Caroline wasn't afraid when the lights went out."

"I think Elizabeth is right," Lila said in her know-it-all voice. "Caroline must be a witch."

Ellen nodded. "I always thought Caroline was kind of strange."

Eva looked over her shoulder. Caroline was

looking right at them. "We'd better be careful," Eva said.

Amy gulped. "We don't want to make Caroline mad," she agreed. "She might zap us into frogs—or worse."

Jessica shuddered. She was glad her friends knew about Caroline, but she was also worried. Halloween was the next day. What would a real witch do on Halloween?

CHAPTER 8

Toil and Trouble

"Walk slowly," Eva whispered. "We don't want to catch up with Caroline."

Eva was coming to the twins' house that afternoon to play. She had ridden the bus home with Elizabeth and Jessica, and now the three girls were letting Caroline walk well ahead of them on the way home from the bus stop. They watched as Caroline let herself in the front door of her house.

"Let's go spy on Caroline," Eva suggested. "I want to see her broom and her magic potion."

"OK," Jessica said. "That means we've got to go to the backyard where nobody will see us. Come on!"

"I don't think this is a good idea," Elizabeth said slowly. "Caroline could be dangerous."

"If she's dangerous, we'd better find out what she's up to," Jessica said. "Halloween is tomorrow. Anything could happen then."

Elizabeth didn't answer.

"Come on, Lizzie," Jessica said. "There're three of us. You aren't afraid, are you?"

Elizabeth nodded. "A little," she admitted.

"Do you think Caroline's going to turn you into a frog like Amy said?" Eva teased. "Or make a big green wart grow on your nose?"

"Well," Elizabeth said. "Sort of."

"You could go home, then," Eva said. "Jessica and I will be back soon. We'll tell you everything we see."

Elizabeth thought for a second. "No," she said. "If you're both going, I'm going, too."

Jessica, Elizabeth, and Eva walked over to the Pearces'. Then, step by careful step, they sneaked into the Pearces' backyard and hid behind the oak tree.

The girls hid for what seemed like forever.

"Nothing's happening," Eva said after a while. "Maybe we should go play at your house."

But then, from the Pearces' garage, Eva, Jessica, and Elizabeth heard someone chanting: "Double, double, toil and trouble! Fire burn, and cauldron bubble!"

"What's that?" Elizabeth whispered.

"Caroline's casting a spell!" Eva whispered back, wide-eyed.

"A *spell*?" Jessica said. She turned pale. "What do we do now?"

Eva pulled on Elizabeth's arm. "We've got to get a closer look."

Jessica pulled on Elizabeth's other arm. "I say we get out of here."

"I want to see," Eva said, pulling harder.

"I want to go home," Jessica said, pulling harder, too.

"Ouch!" Elizabeth said. "You guys are hurting me. Let go!"

Jessica and Eva let go of Elizabeth's arm, but they had made so much noise that Caroline poked her head out of the garage.

"What are you doing here?" she asked, walking right toward the oak tree. "You're spying on me, aren't you?"

Elizabeth gulped. "Are—are you a good witch?"

"No, I'm a wicked witch," Caroline said,

putting her hands on her hips. "The most wicked witch in the whole school! And don't you forget it!"

Elizabeth took a few steps back. Caroline had just admitted that she was a witch!

Eva and Jessica started to back up, too.

"We're really, really sorry, Caroline," Elizabeth managed to say. "We didn't mean to make you mad."

"Well, you'd better watch it. You're no match for me, Elizabeth!" Caroline yelled. "If you're smart, you'll give up now. You can't win!"

Elizabeth turned and ran for her life. Jessica and Eva were right behind her. Elizabeth didn't stop running until she got to her own house. She threw open the door and all three girls rushed in. Jessica locked the door behind them.

"We're in trouble," Elizabeth said. "*Big* trouble."

"I think *you're* in trouble," Eva said. "Caroline told *you* to watch it. She didn't say anything to me or Jessica."

"That's true," Jessica said. "But we'll help protect you from her, Lizzie. Right, Eva?"

Eva looked uncertain. "I think Caroline is a powerful witch—too powerful for us."

Elizabeth started to tremble. "I've got to read my book," she said.

Elizabeth, Eva, and Jessica went up to the twins' bedroom. Elizabeth looked through *All About Witches*, hoping it would tell her what to do about Caroline. But the book didn't say one word about how to protect yourself from an angry witch.

"What do I do now?" Elizabeth asked. She

looked at Jessica and Eva. "I don't want to be a frog."

"We'd better do something fast," Jessica said. "Tomorrow's Halloween."

"I've got an idea," Eva said. "Let's try to remember all the things people in movies do to protect themselves from witches. Then you can do the same thing."

Elizabeth, Jessica, and Eva thought and thought. They could remember movies with werewolves, vampires, and dinosaurs, but they couldn't remember a movie with a witch in it.

The twins were still thinking when Eva went home. They thought through dinner and dessert. They thought in between their homework questions.

"*The Wizard of Oz!*" Elizabeth said suddenly, while she and Jessica were changing

54

into their pajamas. A few minutes later, they had come up with a plan.

"I hope it works," Jessica said as she turned out the light.

"I hope so, too," Elizabeth said with a shiver.

CHAPTER 9

Halloween

Elizabeth and Jessica were waiting at the bus stop. Halloween morning was sunny, but the twins were too worried to be happy about the good weather.

"Where is she?" Jessica asked.

"Probably finishing up a potion," Elizabeth answered.

Jessica knew Caroline might cast a spell on Elizabeth as soon as she showed up. Their plan was ready, but they had to wait for the perfect moment to use it.

In the meantime, Jessica smoothed out the pleated skirt she was wearing, and fingered the "S" and "V" letters sewn onto her sweater. The letters stood for Sweet Valley. Jessica looked just like a cheerleader. Her hair was up in a ponytail, and she held two pompoms in one hand.

Elizabeth had her costume on, too. She was wearing a beige raincoat and one of her grandfather's hats. An oversized magnifying glass and a plastic pipe dangled from a long string around her neck. Elizabeth was dressed like Sherlock Holmes, a famous detective. It was the perfect costume for her because she loved to read mystery stories.

There was something else around Elizabeth's neck. Both she and Jessica were wearing garlic necklaces. That morning Eva had called because she remembered seeing a movie where garlic was used to keep vampires away. Caroline wasn't a vampire, but the twins decided that garlic might work on witches, too.

"Here comes the bus," Elizabeth announced.

Jessica looked up and down the street. There was no sign of Caroline.

"Maybe Caroline is sick," Jessica said. "Maybe we'll be lucky."

Elizabeth nodded. "Or maybe the garlic is working."

At school, Amy, Eva, and Lila were waiting for the twins.

Lila had on a beautiful butterfly costume with colorful wings attached to her back.

Amy was dressed as a dog. Furry ears flopped in her eyes. She was wearing a tag that said "Spot."

"Where's Caroline?" Eva asked. Her clown costume was very colorful. Her shoes were almost a foot long. "Did she do anything to you yet?"

"She wasn't on the bus," Elizabeth said. "Jessica thinks she's sick."

"Sick in the head, you mean," Lila said. She sniffed the air. "Hey, what's that funny smell?"

"Garlic," Jessica said, wrinkling her nose.

Eva told Amy and Lila about how Caroline had caught them spying the afternoon before.

"Wow! What are you going to do, Elizabeth?" Amy said. "Caroline sounds mean."

"Jessica and I have a plan," Elizabeth told them.

"We'll use it if she shows up," Jessica said.

"Maybe Caroline's flying to school," Amy suggested.

At that very moment, Caroline came running into the classroom. She was wearing a long, flowing black dress. Her skin was bright green and her nose seemed extra long.

"Look at her hair," Amy whispered.

Caroline's hair looked redder than ever and it was sticking out in a knotty mess from beneath her tall, pointed black hat.

"I think she *did* fly," Eva whispered.

Jessica crossed her fingers. She hoped Caroline wouldn't cast any spells before they had a chance to try their plan.

"Happy Halloween!" Mrs. Otis said as she walked into the classroom. "I'll take attendance and then it will be time for book reports. Jessica, I'd like you to give yours first."

Jessica frowned and headed to her seat. She didn't ever like to be first when it came to book reports or explaining her science projects. Still, being first meant that she would get it all over with quickly. She walked to the front of the room after Mrs. Otis had finished taking attendance. "My report is on how Halloween started," she announced. "A long, long time ago in England, November first was considered the beginning of the new year. It was also the beginning of winter."

Jessica paused. She saw Caroline lean forward. Did that mean Caroline was getting ready to do something witchy? Jessica didn't wait to find out.

"October thirty-first was a scary day," she continued. "People believed that on this day there was a war between winter and summer. They thought that the army of winter—ghosts, goblins, and witches—grew very strong.

"All the people wanted to protect themselves from the wicked creatures. To do this they built bonfires on hilltops to light up the sky. They also put on masks and animal skins so that they looked frightening. They hoped their costumes would keep the evil creatures from knowing who they were."

Jessica looked around Mrs. Otis's room. She saw a dog, two ghosts, a lion—and one very scary witch. "I guess things haven't changed that much," Jessica finished.

"Very nice, Jessica," Mrs. Otis said. "I don't think many of us knew the origin of Halloween."

Next, Andy, Lois, and Eva gave their reports. Then Mrs. Otis called on Elizabeth.

Elizabeth walked up to the front of the

classroom very slowly. "I read a book on . . . on witches," she said. Her voice was shaky.

Jessica knew Elizabeth was worried about Caroline. And there was something to worry about. Caroline was playing with her red hair and mumbling to herself. Jessica was expecting the worst to happen any second. But she was proud that her sister wasn't letting Caroline scare her into not giving her report.

"That was good," Jessica said when Elizabeth sat down. "Now maybe Caroline will think twice before trying anything."

Elizabeth nodded and listened as the rest of the students gave their reports. Only one person was left.

"Caroline will finish up with a special report about costumes," Mrs. Otis said.

Book Reports

Caroline got up and slowly turned to face the class. She stared right at Elizabeth. Then she stretched her arms out and bared her teeth. "Double, double, toil and trouble—" Caroline chanted.

"Now!" Jessica yelled.

CHAPTER 10

First Place

Jessica and Elizabeth ran to the front of the class.

"Stand back," Elizabeth yelled.

She and Jessica each poured a thermos full of water on Caroline's head.

"Caroline's going to melt," Jessica said. "Just like in *The Wizard of Oz*."

Elizabeth held her breath. Jessica held her breath. But Caroline didn't melt.

"What are you doing?" Caroline demanded. "You got me all wet! My costume is ruined."

"Costume?" Jessica repeated. She looked at Elizabeth.

"What's this all about, girls?" Mrs. Otis asked, looking very surprised.

Elizabeth's face turned red. "We—we thought Caroline was a real witch," she stammered.

Caroline giggled. "Don't be silly. I'm just dressed like a witch for Halloween."

"If you're just a witch for pretend," Jessica said, "that's the best costume I've ever seen."

"I agree," Mrs. Otis said. "That's why I nominate Caroline for the Best Class Costume award. Does anyone else agree?"

"Yes," came shouts from all over the class.

"All right!" Caroline said. "This is great. I really wanted to win."

Jessica and Elizabeth helped Caroline dry off her costume. Then they hurried back to their seats.

Caroline got ready to finish her report.

She stretched her arms out. "Double, double, toil and trouble," Caroline chanted.

"I feel silly," Elizabeth whispered to Jessica.

"I feel relieved," Jessica whispered back.

At recess, everyone crowded around Caroline.

"How did you know about Mrs. Frankel's skeleton?" Elizabeth asked.

"Easy," Caroline said. "I saw Mrs. Frankel throw out the skeleton. It was broken. And I saw her take the ghost out of its plastic wrapping. I put two and two together."

"What about the broom Jessica and Elizabeth saw you with?" Amy asked.

Caroline shrugged. "Sweeping is one of my jobs at home."

"What about that big pot?" Jessica asked.

"That's just the pot my dad uses to make

chili," Caroline said. "I was stirring it for him so it wouldn't burn."

"And the lizard?" Eva asked.

Caroline frowned. "The lizard was supposed to be part of my costume," she explained, "but I didn't bring it because I'm afraid to pick it up."

Everyone laughed.

"What about that spooky chant?" Eva asked.

"It is scary, isn't it?" Caroline said. "My dad taught it to me. It comes from an old play called *Macbeth*. It's by Shakespeare."

"Wow," Elizabeth said, sounding impressed. "I didn't know Shakespeare wrote about stuff like witches."

"How did you get to school this morning?" Amy asked Caroline. "We thought you were flying here on your magic broomstick."

Caroline giggled. "I wish. My mom drove me because I was late. It took a lot of time to get my costume just right."

"What were you doing in Mrs. Frankel's garden?" Jessica asked.

"I was looking for Misty. She got lost." Caroline shivered. "I couldn't wait to get out of there."

Elizabeth let out a big sigh. "I'm glad you're not a witch."

"And I'm glad you're not going to turn Elizabeth into a frog," Jessica said.

"I'm sorry I got mad at you guys," Caroline said. "I thought you were trying to copy my witch costume."

"You did?" Elizabeth said. "Why?"

Caroline shrugged. "You said you were going to be a witch."

"I said I was going to be a lot of things,"

Elizabeth said with a laugh. "I couldn't make up my mind."

"Do you want to come trick-or-treating with us tonight?" Jessica asked.

Caroline smiled. "That sounds great. I'll cast a spell on anyone who doesn't give us loads of candy!"

That evening, a cheerleader, a detective, and a very spooky witch walked down the street together. They rang doorbell after doorbell and soon their bags were starting to fill up.

"Caroline," Jessica said as they headed for the next house. "I dare you to knock on Mrs. Frankel's door."

"I double dare you," Elizabeth said.

Elizabeth, Jessica, and Caroline looked toward Mrs. Frankel's house. The sun had nearly gone down and Mrs. Frankel's yard was full of dancing shadows. The shutters on her house were closed tight. No light shone from inside.

"Maybe she's not home," Caroline said, sounding hopeful.

"Of course she's home," Jessica said. "It's Halloween."

Elizabeth took one of Jessica's hands and one of Caroline's. "Let's knock together."

Caroline, Elizabeth, and Jessica tiptoed up Mrs. Frankel's broken pathway. They reached out and knocked her lion's head knocker.

CRRREEAK! The door swung open. Mrs. Frankel peered out.

"Trick or treat!" Elizabeth, Jessica, and Caroline yelled at the same time.

"Hello there, little ones," Mrs. Frankel

72

said. She was wearing a high-necked white blouse and a long flowing skirt. Her silver hair was twisted up in a knot on top of her head. "Wait right here."

Elizabeth shivered. She didn't want to wait. She wanted to run away as fast as she could. Standing on Mrs. Frankel's doorstep was spooky.

Mrs. Frankel disappeared into the shadows of her hallway and came back with three small bags. The top of each bag was tied with an orange and black ribbon. The sides bulged out. Mrs. Frankel handed one bag to Elizabeth, one to Jessica, and one to Caroline.

"Thank you," the girls said together. Mrs. Frankel smiled. Her teeth glistened in the dark. "I'll be waiting for you next Halloween," she said.

Elizabeth, Jessica, and Caroline looked at each other and then quickly ran down Mrs. Frankel's pathway. They didn't stop until they reached the sidewalk.

"Halloween is the best," Elizabeth said as soon as her heart had slowed down. She opened the bag Mrs. Frankel had given her and smiled when she saw all the treats inside.

"Too bad it's almost over," Caroline added.

"I don't mind," Jessica said, "because if Halloween is almost over that means it'll be Thanksgiving soon."

Elizabeth rubbed her stomach. "Yummy! I love turkey."

"And mashed potatoes," Jessica added.

Caroline rattled her trick-or-treat bag. "Maybe we'll have Halloween candy for dessert on Thanksgiving."

"No way," Jessica said. "Our mom always makes an apple pie and a rhubarb pie for dessert on Thanksgiving. It's a tradition."

Elizabeth licked her lips. "I can hardly wait!"

Will the Wakefields really have a traditional Thanksgiving? Find out in Sweet Valley Kids #34, THE BEST THANKSGIVING EVER.